For my wife, Pam,
and our kids Taylor and Nik:
Thanks for putting up with my long hours
writing and drawing, and occasionally flyfishing.

Special thanks
go out to the following people who made this book possible:

Mike Doherty,
for your contributions to the story.

Marc Chapman,
for tying the flies featured at the end of the book.

Scott Thompson Photography
for the photos of the flies.

Olive the Little Woolly Bugger
Text and Illustrations copyright 2007 by Kirk Werner
All Rights Reserved

No part of this publication may be reproduced in whole or in part, or stored
in a retrieval system, or transmitted in any form or by any means, electronic, mechanical,
photocopying, recording, or otherwise, without written permission by the publisher.

For information contact:
Johnson Books, a Big Earth Publishing company
3005 Center Green Drive, Suite 225, Boulder, Colorado 80301
1-800-258-5830
Email: books@bigearthpublishing.com • www.bigearthpublishing.com

9 8 7 6 5 4

Library of Congress information on file
ISBN 978-1-55566-432-9
Printed in the United States of America by CGX Publishing Solutions

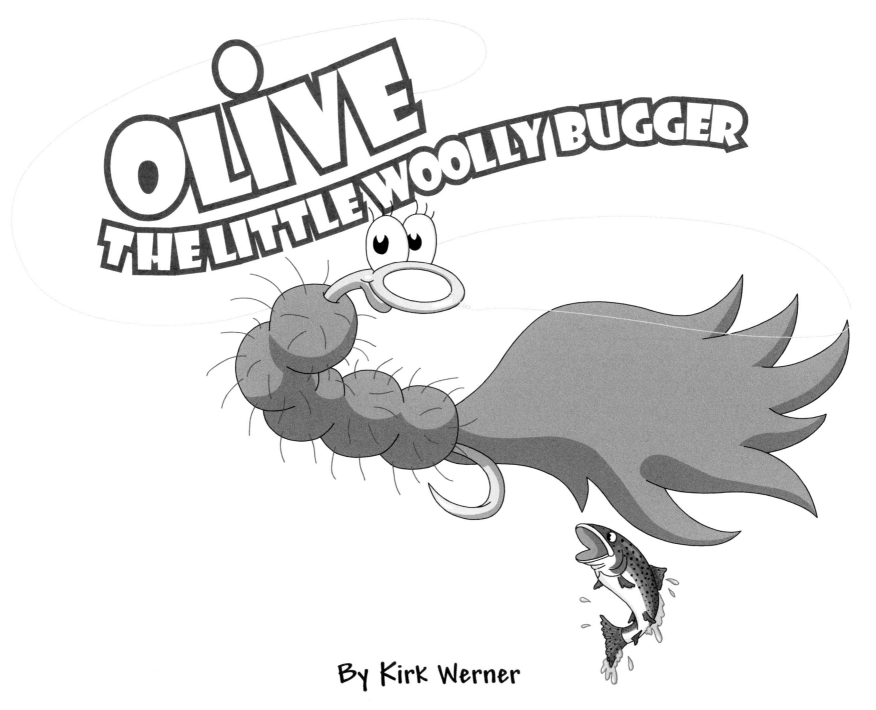

OLIVE
THE LITTLE WOOLLY BUGGER

By Kirk Werner

JOHNSON BOOKS

BOULDER

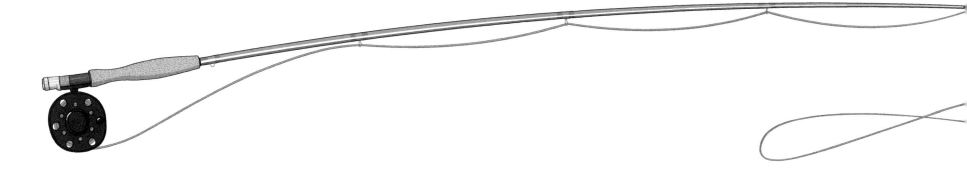

Foreword

Flyfishing is an adventure that includes time spent outdoors with family and friends, fish, equipment, flies, traveling to new places, and learning new things every time you go out.

I started my flyfishing adventure before I was three years old. As a very young boy I learned to tie flies with my dad. The first fly that I learned to tie was the Woolly Bugger. This book had special interest for me because the story is about the flyfishing adventures of a young Woolly Bugger named Olive. One of the most important things to me is to share my love of flyfishing with kids, adults, and families. When I first started, there were very few books for kids to read to learn about flyfishing. It is great to see that Kirk Werner realized there was a need for more kids' flyfishing books and that he shares my passion for this great sport. This book is filled with many of the special things we need to know about flyfishing. All the fun and excitement in this book is shown in unique and colorful illustrations. You will feel like you are right there with Olive living her flyfishing adventure.

If you are looking for a fun-filled story book that will interest kids, adults, or the entire family, then *Olive the Little Woolly Bugger* is the perfect book. Whether you flyfish or not, this book will make you hungry to learn more about flyfishing.

—TYLER BEFUS
Montrose, Colorado

Tyler Befus is eleven years old and has been flyfishing since he was old enough to go along in a child backpack. He started fly casting and fly tying at the age of three and landed his first fly-caught trout on his own shortly before his third birthday. He is the youngest member of the Ross Reels, St. Croix Rod, Rio Products, Inc., Haber Vision, Simms Fishing Products, and Whiting Farms pro staff teams, and is a Signature Fly designer for Umpqua Feather Merchants. Tyler frequently presents kids' flyfishing programs at numerous flyfishing shows around the country and is the youngest fly tier presenting at the International Fly Tying Symposium in Somerset, New Jersey. He has fished the Rocky Mountain region extensively for trout and warmwater species, and his fishing travels have taken him to Alaska for northern pike and sheefish, as well as Japan for Yamame, Iwanna, and Japanese sea bass. Tyler has written two books, *A Kid's Guide to Flyfishing*, and *A Kid's Guide to Fly Tying*, and is working on a kid's flyfishing instructional DVD. He currently holds International Game Fish Association (IFGA) Junior World Records for sheefish and kokanee salmon. His other interests include competing on the Montrose Marlin swim team, playing soccer, hockey and football, piano, theater, photography and drawing. This young fanatic angler lives in Montrose, Colorado, with his mom and dad and three younger sisters.

"**D**on't worry, Olive, you'll do just fine," said her mom as she fussed with Olive's feathers. "Now hurry along, you don't want to be late to your first day of flyfishing camp!" Olive gave her mom a big hug and headed out the door with her backpack.

With her fluffy tail flowing behind her, Olive skipped off. This was a very special day. Ever since Olive could remember, her parents had talked of the day she would go to Camp Tightloops and learn to catch fish. She wanted nothing more than to make them proud.

As Olive came to the bridge that crossed The Big Stream, she paused to look down at the smooth, deep waters. The current was lazy here, and she thought she saw a fish but wasn't sure. After all, she'd only seen pictures of them on the wall of her dad's den. But where The Big Stream started in the far-off mountains, it was a wild and free-flowing river that rushed through lush forests. And up there it was full of fish. Fish called Trout. Olive had learned all this from listening to stories about The Big Stream and of the big ones that lived in its cold, clear, fast-running waters.

"Someday," thought Olive, as she peered over the side of the bridge, "I'm gonna catch a whole bunch of you." She gazed into the dark green water, hoping to see a trout, but there were just big shadows.

When she arrived at Camp Tightloops Olive was amazed by what she saw. Everywhere she looked colorful flies were making their way to class. There were vibrant red-hackled flies, and beautiful pink-winged flies, and big purple flies with shiny bead heads. She even saw a fly that looked like a rainbow! There were very large flies with bodies like jelly-beans, and small flies with bodies that were thin like spaghetti, and everything in between. In fact there were some flies so tiny it was hard to imagine a fish being able to see them!

Olive was sure that fish would really like them all. "They're so beautiful!" she thought. Every one of them looked perfectly tied. The dazzling colors, feathers, and materials made her wonder if she was colorful enough. She was sort of ordinary looking. Her olive-colored feathers had no sparkle or flash, and Olive wondered how she would be able to catch the attention of a hungry fish.

As the flies darted about in all directions, Olive passed by a group of flies standing in a tight circle, talking. They didn't all look the same, but they all had hairs sticking up like a porcupine. As Olive admired them, one of the flies glared at her. Soon the entire group turned to look at her.

"Hi," she said shyly.

"Don't talk to us," shouted one of the flies.

"Yeah, we're dry flies!" yelled another.

"You're not one of us, so SCRAM!" said another in a very unfriendly tone.

The dry flies turned their backs to Olive. She was confused as she walked away because she didn't even know what a dry fly was—she thought all flies were the same. Just then she heard another voice say, "Don't mind them. They think they're better than everyone else."

Olive turned to see something that looked like a ball of dust smiling at her.

"Hi, I'm Gilbert the Gold-Ribbed Hare's Ear," said the small brownish ball of dust.

"My name is Olive," she replied. "Nice to meet you, Gilbert the Gold-Ribbed Hare's Ear."

Olive stared a little harder. He wasn't really a ball of dust so much as a clump of short brown tail feathers and tan fur that made him look like he was wearing a big sweater. He was wrapped in thin strands of gold ribbing. While he wasn't very colorful, he was sure nice, and Olive liked him instantly. Gilbert told Olive that he was a nymph pattern. She didn't know what a nymph was, nor had Olive ever seen a fly quite like Gilbert.

"The dry flies usually keep to their own kind," Gilbert told Olive, "so I just ignore them." Olive still didn't know what a dry fly was, but she decided she would just ignore them, too. The bell rang, and Gilbert and Olive made their way to their classroom.

"Please be seated," said a large, rough looking fly standing at the front of the classroom. "My name is Mr. Muddler Minnow, and I'm your instructor here at Camp Tightloops."

He had obviously done a lot of fishing in his life, because some of his feathers were bent or even broken off. His cone-shaped head was scruffy looking, and his hook showed a small tint of rust. Olive thought he was old and scary looking, but she could also tell that he knew a lot about flyfishing. Olive listened nervously when he spoke.

"Camp Tightloops has a long history of producing some of the finest fishing flies in the land. As your instructor, it's my job to make sure you learn how to catch, and release, wild trout," he continued. "It's every fly's dream to make it to The Big Stream, but first you have to earn a spot in The Fly Box. It takes a lot of practice if you hope to become a fishing fly. Let's start by going around the room and introducing ourselves. We'll start with you," said Mr. Muddler Minnow, pointing to a very fancy-looking fly that appeared to be tied from many different types of materials. His body was wrapped in bright red thread, and he had two large wings that were as white as snow. When the fly stood up to introduce himself, Olive recognized him from the group of mean dry flies in the hallway.

"I'm Randal the Royal Coachman. I'm a dry fly, and dry flies are the best. I can be used in many situations to attract trout of all types. I have a proud family tradition of catching fish, and every year someone from my family makes it into The Fly Box," he boasted.

"How about you?" said Mr. Muddler Minnow, looking at a small fly who was about the same color as Olive.

"My name is Billy the Blue-Winged Olive," said the delicate little fly (aside from color, he looked nothing like Olive). "I look just like a real mayfly, and I guarantee I'll catch fish on cloudy days!" he said with a confidence that impressed Olive.

Then there was Pete the Prince Nymph. He was certainly a wonderful looking fly with his sharp forked tail and small white wings. He had a shiny bead at the end of his body that shone in the light. He was sort of cocky, saying "I'm the finest of all the nymph patterns when it comes to catching trout." Pete went on to tell the class how nymphs were the best flies because they drift in the current, bouncing along the bottom of a stream where trout gobble them up.

"So that's what a nymph is!" Olive thought. "I'm glad I'm not a nymph —I don't think I'd like all that bouncing!"

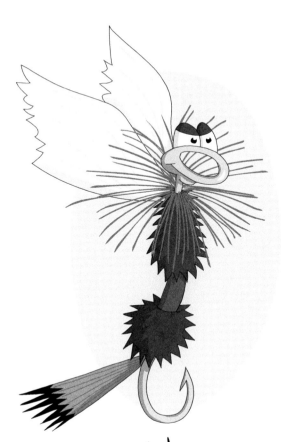

Randal
the Royal Coachman

Billy
the Blue-Winged Olive

Pete
the Prince Nymph

Zachary Zonker was an amazing looking fly with long, fluffy, purple wings made of rabbit fur! His sparkling body looked as if it was made of pearls, and when he spoke, everyone listened. "I'm a streamer fly. I'm designed to look like a small fish that big fish want to eat." Wow! Olive never imagined there were fish that looked like that!

Seated near the front of the room was a very simple looking, but pretty fly with a slender orange body. She spoke in a voice as soft as her downy feathers. "Hello, my name is Polly the Partridge and Orange, and I'm a soft hackle wet fly. I'm made to look like an insect under the water." Partridge feathers were used to tie her hackles, and Olive thought Polly would probably catch fish just because she was so polite!

Suddenly a large and brightly colored dry fly jumped up and yelled, "My name is Stan the Stimulator!!!" This startled nearly everyone in class except for Mr. Muddler Minnow, who calmly said, "There's no need to yell, Stan. Please have a seat."

Olive listened as more dry flies introduced themselves. There was Sally the Yellow Sally, Andy the Adams, and Ernie the Elk Hair Caddis. As the introductions continued, so did the bragging.

Zachary
Zonker

Ernie
the Elk Hair Caddis

Stan
the Stimulator

Sally
the Yellow Sally

Andy
the Adams

Polly
the Partridge & Orange

Olive's thoughts drifted as she pondered the many sizes, shapes, and colors of her classmates, and once again she thought about her own drab-colored feathers. Would a big hungry fish really chase her when there were all of these more colorful, fancy looking flies to choose from? She was startled when Gilbert the Gold-Ribbed Hare's Ear, who was seated behind her, tapped Olive on the back and whispered, "PSST! Hey, Olive—it's your turn."

Olive sat up straight in her chair, embarrassed that she hadn't been paying attention.

"Now then," said Mr. Muddler Minnow, looking directly at Olive, "What's your name?"

"Um, I'm Olive, sir. Olive the Woolly Bugger," she said timidly.

The class erupted in laughter, and a dry fly yelled out, "A Woolly what?!"

Randal chuckled, "Ha-ha! A Woolly Booger!"

Olive slumped in her chair, her feelings terribly hurt. Mr. Muddler Minnow told the class to quiet down. "Thank you, Olive," he said in a kind voice. Tears filled her eyes, and Olive was so upset that she didn't even try to tell the class how good she was going to be at catching trout. After all, she hadn't even seen a real live fish before, so she had nothing to boast about.

That night in her bunk Olive dreamed she was floating quietly on the surface of a beautiful river. All around her big trout were rising and jumping, munching on flies.

The next morning she awoke from her dream excited and happy to start another day at Camp Tightloops. She didn't care if the other flies laughed at her or made fun of her name. She was going to earn a spot in The Fly Box, and she was going to make it to The Big Stream, where she was going to catch fish. Olive just knew it!

In the days that followed, Mr. Muddler Minnow taught the class all about flyfishing and showed them a dazzling assortment of equipment. There were fly rods in many lengths and sizes (some were even made of bamboo!), and as many various reels that matched all the different rods. There were fly lines in an assortment of colors (Olive thought she liked the olive-colored ones best, but she learned that color didn't really matter so much). She discovered that some fly lines floated, while the tips of some sank a little bit. There were even some lines that sank completely to the bottom! Olive's eyes grew wide as she pondered what it must look like at the bottom of a deep stream.

Tied to the end of the fly line was a very thin, clear line called a leader, and this is what the flies would be tied to when they went fishing. There were different sizes of leader used for different sizes of flies and fish. The tip of the leader was called a tippet, which Olive thought was a funny word. At first it was all a bit confusing to Olive, but she listened carefully. Mr. Muddler Minnow told them how dry flies were used to imitate insects resting on the surface of the water, while nymphs, wet flies, and streamers were made to look like bugs or small fish underneath the surface of the water. Olive was pretty sure she wanted to be a dry fly so she could float on the surface.

The first day of swimming practice was very exciting. As they gathered around the edge of the practice pool, one by one the flies hopped into the water. The nymphs bobbed along on the bottom, while a few wet flies dove in and swam around under the water's surface. Olive's friend Polly the Partridge and Orange was very graceful, and her soft hackles flowed gently as she swam. With their bushy hackles, the dry flies all floated like corks as they paddled on top of the water, splashing each other and having fun among themselves.

"Hey, that's cool!" said Olive. "Look at me—I'm a dry fly— *Cowabunga!*" she yelled as she jumped into the pool with a big splash and slowly began to sink. She struggled to the surface, drenched and coughing.

There was a chorus of laughter from the dry flies. "Hey, the Woolly Booger floats just like a rock!" said that mean old Randal.

Mr. Muddler Minnow helped her from the pool and said, "Olive, don't worry—not every fly is supposed to float."

Olive stood there, dripping wet and embarrassed. But she remembered what Gilbert had told her and ignored the teasing. "So what if I can't float yet," thought Olive. "I'll learn to float, and I'll catch fish!"

Next, the flies learned about flying. In order to get to the water, a fly had to be cast. Mr. Muddler Minnow drew pictures of how a fly rod tossed the line back and forth when casting flies to waiting fish. He told them that it was very important to relax and let the rod carry the line in tight loops on both the forward and backward casts.

Another very important thing they learned about was presentation.

"Pre-sen-ta-tion," Olive sounded out the word in her head.

"Presentation is when a fly lands on the water after being cast," said Mr. Muddler Minnow. "Fishing flies—particularly dry flies—need to land gently so they don't scare fish when they're feeding on the surface." While the flies would not actually be cast with a fly rod until they earned a trip to the The Big Stream, they were given a chance to feel what it was like.

One at a time they were each tied onto the end of the thin leader and then swung back and forth over the water. The dry flies seemed to float in the air just like they floated on the water, touching down on the surface and barely making a ripple. Gilbert the Gold-Ribbed Hare's Ear landed with a gentle splash, but he was so small that Olive hardly noticed his ripples. "Way to go, Gilbert!" Olive called out from the side of the pool.

"Olive, it's your turn," said Mr. Muddler Minnow.

As she was tied to the end of the leader, Olive took a couple of deep breaths. "OK, I'm ready," she said. Startled and wide-eyed at the end of the line, she swung wildly back and forth and soon grew very dizzy. Without warning Olive slapped down with a big splash. Ripples went out in all directions as she lay stunned on the surface of the water. She slowly began to sink, which helped to drown out the roars of laughter coming from the edge of the pool. Down, down, down she sank, holding her breath.

All of a sudden she felt herself being tugged toward the edge of the pool. Olive tried to resist, but as the line was pulled in, she relaxed. And then she actually began to move gracefully at the end of the leader, her bushy tail wiggling back and forth. As she was pulled from the water, a group of dry flies pointed at Olive and laughed.

"Hey, Olive—nice belly flop!" said a familiar voice. It was Randal again.

"Yeah, and after you sank, what was all that wiggling?" shouted Andy as he looked at the other flies. "It looked like you were drowning!" They all laughed at poor Olive.

Olive stood there, dripping wet. "Hey, don't listen to them," Gilbert said. "Yeah, you'll get better at this," added Polly. Olive saw Mr. Muddler Minnow approaching, and she knew what he was going to say.

"I'm sorry, sir," she apologized. "I made an awful big splash out there, and—"

"Olive, you did just great," said Mr. Muddler Minnow.

Without hesitation Olive continued, "And I didn't float very well, either, and I wiggled a lot when I swam, and ..."

Suddenly Olive realized what he had said. "I did great, sir?"

"You're not designed for delicate presentation," said Mr. Muddler Minnow. "Olive, you, my friend, are not at all like those floating showboats known as dry flies. You are a streamer, and streamers are supposed to swim like small fish, zipping and darting here and there. Can you zip and dart? Let me show you what I mean."

Much to the surprise of everyone, Mr. Muddler Minnow dove into the water and began swimming very quickly in all directions just like a small fish. And just as quickly as he'd zipped and darted, he emerged from the water, dripping wet and breathing hard. Everybody laughed, including Mr. Muddler Minnow himself. "That, class, is how you zip and dart!" Looking directly at the group of dry flies who had taunted Olive, he asked, "Anyone care to give it a try?"

Randal and the others stood there trembling and shaking their heads. "N-n-no, sir," they replied (dry flies get very upset when they get too wet and stop floating). Then Randal muttered under his breath, "I could if I wanted to, but I don't want to."

"Randal, did you have something to say?" asked Mr. Muddler Minnow in a very stern voice.

Randal said nothing.

"It's OK if you make a little splash, Olive," added Mr. Muddler Minnow. "The fish you're going to catch won't see you land anyway, because they're deep in the water. With more practice you'll learn to relax, and your splashes will get smaller. Now go dry off, and we'll see you tomorrow morning," he said.

Over the next few days, the flies spent more time practicing their presentation. The dry flies sailed ever so gracefully at the end of the leader, landing gently on the water. They got so good at it that they no longer made even tiny ripples on the surface. And Olive got better, too. She still landed not so gently, but her splashes did get smaller. And she continued to sink and swim gracefully, zipping and darting, just like a small fish. Her zipping and darting fascinated the others, and Olive soon made friends with all the flies except Randal, who continued to glare at her. She no longer paid any attention to him, but instead went about her business of learning to be a fishing fly. Olive was learning many new things, and she looked forward to each new day.

There was one day in particular that Olive and the other new flies dreaded: Barbless Hook Day. Mr. Muddler Minnow had taught the campers that it was very important when fishing for wild trout that the fish be released uninjured. He explained about the sharp little barbs at the ends of their hooks and that by having the barbs flattened, their hooks could be removed from a fish's mouth much more easily, without injuring the fish.

"Do you guys think this will hurt?" Olive whispered to Gilbert and Polly.

Her friends just shrugged and looked nervous. The flies lined up, and one at a time they stood very still while their barbs were pinched flat with small pliers. When it was Olive's turn, she closed her eyes and held her breath. Before she knew it she was done. "Hey, that didn't hurt at all!" said Olive. She was glad for that, and she was also glad that her barb wouldn't be able to hurt a fish some day.

On the final day at Camp Tightloops, Olive and all the other flies could feel the excitement in the air. Tomorrow was the first day of fishing season, and a dozen new flies would be added to The Fly Box in time for a trip to The Big Stream. Mr. Muddler Minnow spoke at their graduation ceremony.

"It's my honor to announce the newest flies that have been selected for The Fly Box this season." Mr. Muddler Minnow read from a list of the very best flies. One by one Olive heard their familiar names. The dry flies hopped proudly to the front of the room and stood in line.

The names of more flies were called, including her friends Polly and Gilbert. Everyone applauded including Olive, although it was hard to hide her disappointment. She had worked so hard and tried her very best. While she never did learn to float, she learned to zip and dart underwater. Even her splashes had gotten smaller. As Olive's eyes filled with tears, she heard Mr. Muddler Minnow's voice once again, "And Olive the Woolly Bugger. Congratulations everyone!"

"What? Me?!" she said out loud.

The room erupted with applause, and Olive was so overcome with joy that she nearly tripped over her flowing tail feathers as she hurried to join the others in line. The only fly in the room who wasn't clapping was Randal, who sat in his chair with his head held low. Randal hadn't been selected, and even though he'd never been nice to Olive, she felt bad for him.

"Now remember," added Mr. Muddler. "Earning a spot in The Fly Box is a big honor, but it's not the end of your journey. If you want to stay in The Fly Box, you have to prove you can catch fish. Now go out there and make us all proud!"

When her parents finally found Olive among the large crowd, they gave her a great big hug. "We're so proud of you, Olive," said her mother as she fussed with Olive's feathers.

Her dad smiled, "We knew you could do it!"

Marching single file, the newly selected flies headed toward what was the most magnificent thing Olive had ever seen. The Fly Box was finely constructed of rich, dark wood. Carved into the lid was a beautiful image of a leaping trout. The wood had a sweet smell to it, and Olive couldn't wait to climb in. Peering inside the box, she saw rows of older flies, all headed back to The Big Stream for another season. The veterans looked very serious as they stared down at the new arrivals.

"New flies start in the bottom row," Mr. Muddler Minnow had told them. "If you want to get to the top row, first you have to catch fish." The older flies watched silently as Olive took her spot next to Gilbert and Polly. She glanced around nervously.

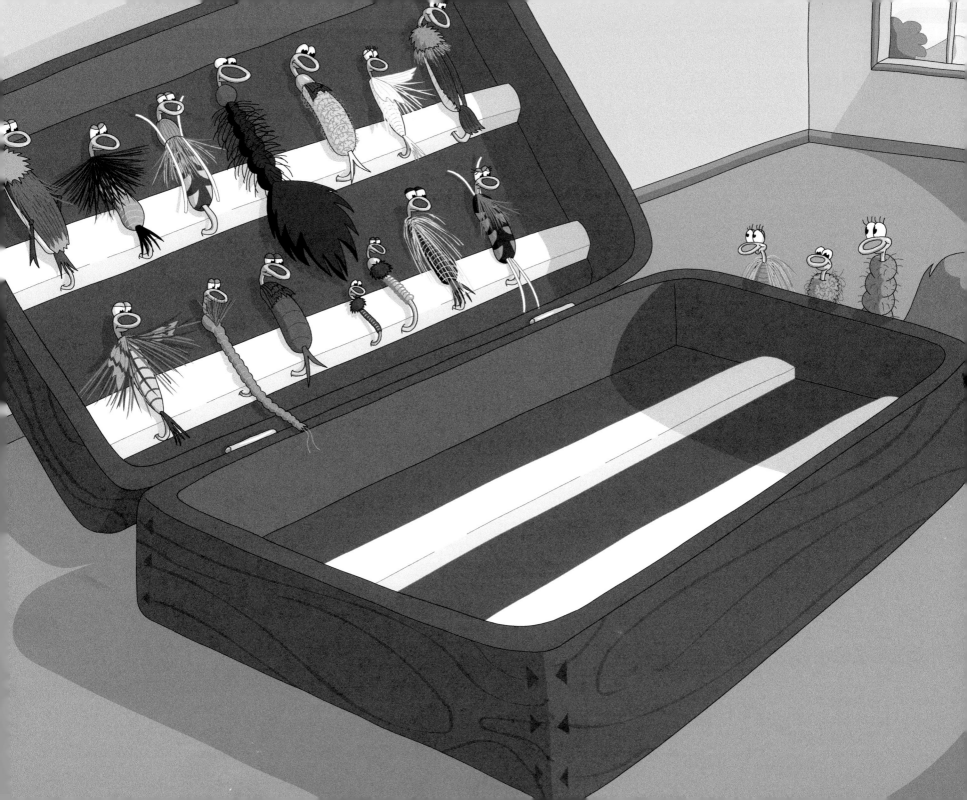

"Don't worry, Olive," said a familiar voice from above. "You deserve to be here." In all the excitement, Olive hadn't even noticed him in the very top row.

"Mr. Muddler Minnow! What are you doing in here?" asked Olive. She was surprised and very glad to see her instructor!

"One last trip before I retire," he said. "Besides, I have to see how well my campers do when it comes to actually catching fish." Mr. Muddler Minnow smiled at Olive just as the lid to The Fly Box closed. And then it was dark and quiet. Olive took a deep breath of the sweet smelling air.

"Mmmm…" she said happily, "I like it in here!" As Olive settled into her spot in The Fly Box she thought about everything she'd learned at Camp Tightloops. Although it hadn't been easy, and at times she had wanted to quit, it was worth the effort. Here she was—Olive the little Woolly Bugger—on her way to The Big Stream!

The End

These hand-tied fishing flies represent some of the characters from the story. They are just a small sampling of some of the better known fly patterns available. There are countless patterns used around the world, and fly anglers will discover slight variations in the same pattern depending on who tied them. Many people make up their own patterns, too!

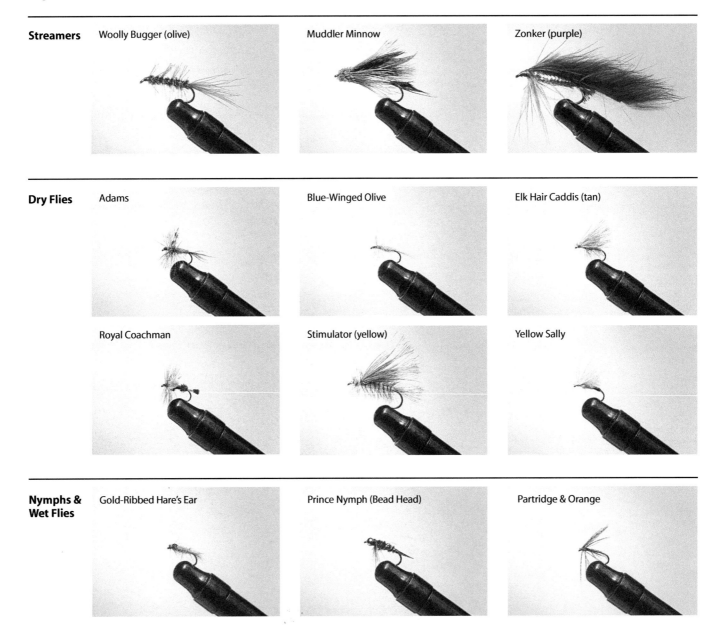

Streamers Woolly Bugger (olive)   Muddler Minnow   Zonker (purple)

Dry Flies Adams   Blue-Winged Olive   Elk Hair Caddis (tan)

Royal Coachman   Stimulator (yellow)   Yellow Sally

Nymphs & Wet Flies Gold-Ribbed Hare's Ear   Prince Nymph (Bead Head)   Partridge & Orange

Catch the next Olive book and reel it in!

Your children will get hooked on flyfishing with the help of Olive and a colorful cast of characters. From earning a coveted spot in The Fly Box to catching (and releasing) a wild trout in The Big Stream, Olive discovers that everyone has a special purpose in life. Featuring eye-catching illustrations, delightful dialogue and kid-friendly facts, this series will make a big splash with flyfishing fans everywhere.

KIRK WERNER never set out to become a children's book author. While he has always enjoyed writing, it is his love of flyfishing and illustrating that led him to create the story of Olive the Woolly Bugger. He is a homegrown product of Washington state, where he lives with his wife and two kids and one itchy dog. He has more stories planned for Olive the Woolly Bugger so stay tuned.

1: Olive the Little Woolly Bugger

2: Olive and The Big Stream

3: Olive Goes For a Wild Ride